KU-154-205

This is Ivan, the oldest and bossiest ghost-hunter.

This is Midge, the smallest ghost-hunter ever.

This is Ellie, who has the sharpest eyes.

The three children peered out of the window as their train pulled into the station.

Ivan was so keen to start ghost-hunting that he jumped off first.

The platform was crowded with people. "Do you know what your Aunt Lavender looks like?" asked Ivan.

"No, but Dad said she has red hair, always wears something spotty and often wears shoes that don't match," replied Ellie.

 Can you help the children find Aunt Lavender?

Aunt Lavender drove at top speed to Trembly Towers. It was the spookiest house the children had ever seen.

"Come in and make yourselves at home," she said, and they followed her into the hall.

This is how the hall looked before Ellie felt the tap ...

8

Suddenly Ellie felt a tap on her shoulder, but when she turned round there was no one to be seen.

When Ellie turned back again she noticed that five things had disappeared!

 Can you spot which five things were missing from the hall?

and this is how it looked afterwards.

9

Ellie wanted to tell the others, but Aunt Lavender was showing them where their bedroom was.

It turned out to be at the very top of a long, dark, twisting staircase.

The door creaked as they opened it...

BANG! It slammed shut behind them and all the lights went out. The flickering fire threw spooky shadows on the walls.

 Can you work out what is making each of the four spooky shapes?

The three children did not sleep well that night.

They were still tired when they went downstairs to breakfast.

"Go into the dining-room and help yourselves," bustled Aunt Lavender.

As they went in, Midge immediately noticed that things were not quite as they should be.

Can you spot six things on the table that are in the wrong place?

13

"This is spooky!" said Ivan. "It's time for us to start looking for the ghost of Trembly Towers."

They began their search in the reading room.

Their luck was in! On the desk was a letter from the ghost, but it was very puzzling.

Can you help the children solve the puzzle?

Dear Ghost Hunters,
Here are four of my favourite hiding places.

BEDROOM

GARDEN SHED

HALL

STUDY

To find where I am today, look out for five things in the reading room that don't belong. Collect them up and take them to the right hidey-hole. See you soon!

Ghost

"Got it!" shouted Ellie. "We must take all these garden things back to the shed."

"And then we'll see the ghost!" said Ivan. "Come on, this way!"

The children raced outside.

But the Trembly Towers garden turned out to be a maze and they didn't know which way to go.

Can you lead the children along the paths to the shed? They mustn't cross the puddles.

When they finally made it to the shed they were very hot and bothered.

They crept in hoping to meet the ghost. There was no sign of it anywhere.

The children turned to go, but they couldn't open the door. Someone or something had locked them in!

"Let's hurry up and find a way out," said Ellie. "This place is creepy." Then she noticed that Midge had found five large keys.

 Which key will open the shed door?

Free from the shed, they ran to tell Aunt Lavender. "That sounds like Spook, the butler," she said.

"He worked here a hundred years ago. Now he haunts Trembly Towers, and tries to frighten my visitors."

"Would you like to see him?"
The children nodded.

Aunt Lavender told them to collect up ten spiders from the kitchen.

 Can you help the children find ten spiders?

Next, Aunt Lavender told them to let the spiders go in the study, and to watch the rocking chair.

The spiders crept across the carpet and the rocking chair started to move. Then, suddenly...

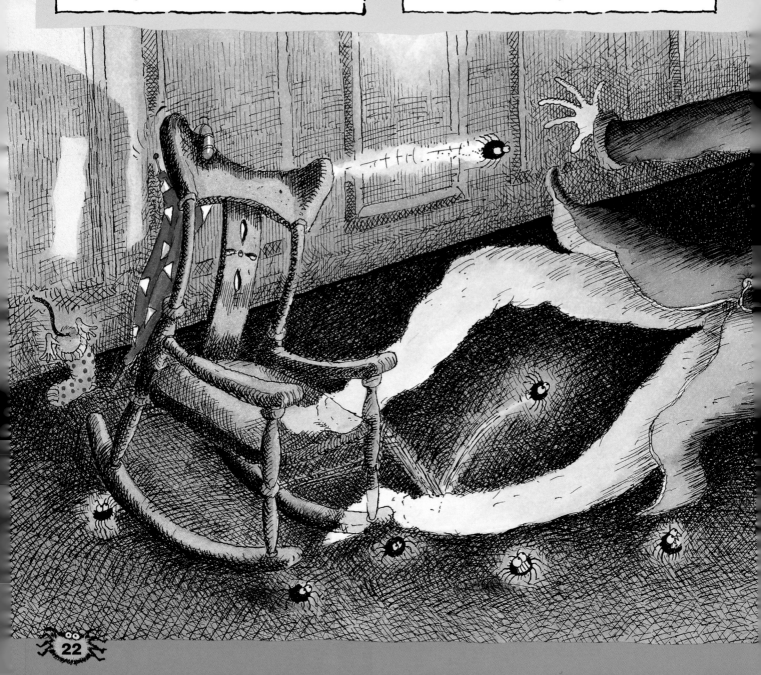

"Yowwl!" The ghost of Trembly Towers leapt into the air in horror and the children gasped. They had already seen Spook twice on their adventures!

 Can you remember where they saw him?

Spook didn't trouble the children after that, except when they played hide-and-seek, and he couldn't resist joining in.

Goodbye and thank you for helping us find the ghost.

Look for these things in every big picture:

One piece of Aunt Lavender's pink washing. She put a red scarf in with the white washing by mistake and everything turned pink.

Either Howl the dog or Screech the cat. They both prowl around the Towers, but are never seen together.

Under this flap, and the one on page 4, you'll find lots of extra things to spot in the big pictures.

When you have finished reading the story, open out the flaps and start searching!

The Answers

- The answers to the story puzzles are shown with single black lines.

- The answers to the fun flap puzzles are shown with double black lines.

Pages 4 and 5

Pages 6 and 7

Spook

Pages 8 and 9

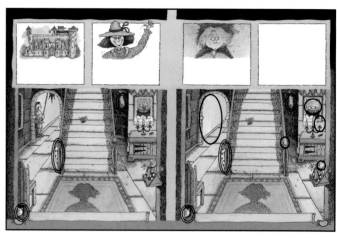

Pages 10 and 11

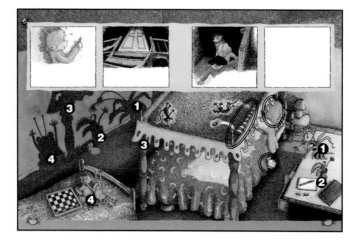

Pages 12 and 13

Pages 14 and 15

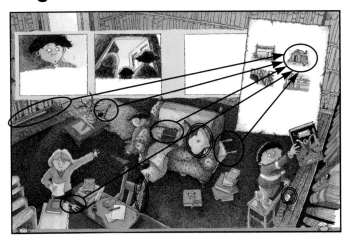

Pages 16 and 17

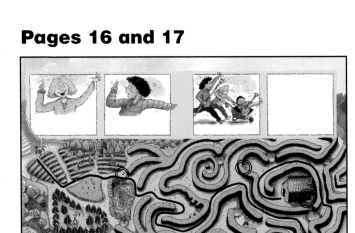

Spook

Pages 18 and 19

Pages 20 and 21

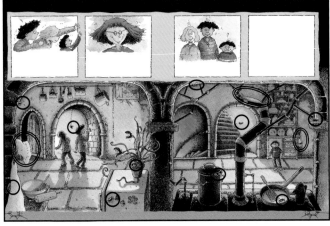

Pages 22 and 23

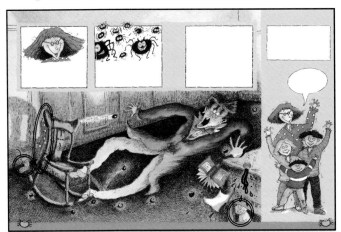

25